AF341989

Taxes and Government Spending

Taxes and Government Spending

Andrea Lubov

Series Editor: M. Barbara Killen
Professor, University of Minnesota

Lerner Publications Company ■ Minneapolis, Minnesota

Page 2: *The Metropolitan Museum of Art. Governments often provide money to support the arts.*

Words that appear in **bold** type are listed in a glossary that starts on page 83.

Library of Congress Cataloging-in-Publication Data

Lubov, Andrea.
    Taxes and government spending / Andrea Lubov.

        p.   cm.—(Economics for today)
    Includes index.
    Summary: Describes how federal, state, and local governments tax citizens, the different kinds of taxes, and how tax revenues are spent. Also explains how federal spending affects the national economy and discusses the federal deficit.
    1. Taxation—United States—Juvenile literature. 2. Government spending policy—United States—Juvenile literature. 3. Fiscal policy—United States—Juvenile literature. 4. Budget deficits—United States—Juvenile literature. [1. Taxation. 2. Government spending policy. 3. Fiscal policy. 4. Budget deficits.]
    I. Title. II. Series.

HJ2381.L83   1990   336.2'00973—dc20   89-12470
ISBN 0-8225-1777-9 (lib. bdg.)   CIP
                                                                          AC

Manufactured in the United States of America

1 2 3 4 5 6 7 8 9 10 99 98 97 96 95 94 93 92 91 90

CONTENTS

1 Governments in the United States   7

2 What Should a Good Tax System
  Be Like?   20

3 A Closer Look at Smith's Principles   29

4 Taxes in the United States   38

5 How Governments Spend Their Money   49

6 The Federal Government Deficit   60

7 Can Government Spending Make
  a Difference?   70

Glossary   83

Index   86

GOVERNMENTS IN THE UNITED STATES

Do you remember the first time you went to the store to buy something—such as a candy bar or a comic book? You probably gave the clerk as much money as the marked price, and then you discovered that the item cost a few cents more. Those extra few cents were for something called the *sales tax.* Delaware, Montana, New Hampshire, and Oregon do not have any sales tax, so if you live in one of these states, you probably have not paid this tax. If you do live in one of these states and have bought something in another state, weren't you surprised at the extra cost?

The sales tax is one of several kinds of taxes that United States citizens pay to support their governments. **Taxation** supports about 82,300 governments in the United States, including the federal, state, and local governments. Local governments are governments in areas that are smaller than states, such as cities, counties, townships, and school districts. Each of the 82,300 governments in the United States does something for the citizens it serves.

You and your family almost certainly pay taxes to at least five, but probably no more than eight or ten, different governments. Everyone pays taxes to the federal government, their state government, their county, their school district, and their city, town, village, or township. You might also pay taxes to at least one special local government, such as an electric district, a fire control district, or a library district. These special local governments usually provide only one service, but most other governments tax people and businesses that they serve in order to provide many different services.

Federal, state, and local governments give us goods and services that we cannot buy in stores. Goods and services that we can buy in stores are produced by private businesses.

Most private businesses would not be able to earn any money if they tried to sell the kinds of goods and services that governments provide. Many of the things that governments provide, such as education in a public school, are available at no charge to everyone who wants to use that service. Even though people who use such things as schools and police services do not pay to use them, these services are not really "free." Instead, the

The United States Postal Service delivers letters and packages to every household in the country. A private business probably wouldn't be able to deliver all the mail in the United States efficiently and affordably. Citizens pay taxes so that the U.S. postal system can provide this service at a reasonable cost.

If you wanted to visit Yellowstone National Park, you might have to pay a small fee to enter. But this entrance fee would not provide enough money for the government to maintain the park and protect its land and wildlife. The federal government makes up the difference with tax dollars.

people who use government services pay for them indirectly through taxes. For some government services, like admission to a national park, there is also a small charge, which is called a user fee.

Many of the people who use the goods and services that governments provide, such as roads and public hospitals, could not afford to buy these things if they had to pay for them individually. It would be impossible to decide how much to charge each person for some government services. At the same time, most people agree that the goods and services that governments provide are important and necessary. To be certain that the necessary goods and services are available to those who need them, people and businesses pay taxes to the federal, state, and local governments, which in turn provide the services.

Sometimes you may not even realize you are getting something a government provides. Factories and mines, for example, are much safer places than they were in the early part of this century, because the federal government and many state governments have passed laws that require businesses to pay attention to the safety of their employees. There is no way for you to buy a safe workplace all by yourself, but by taxing *everyone,* the government helps prevent a number of work-related accidents.

In this book we will look at the goods and services that governments provide and the kinds of taxes that businesses and people pay to get these goods and services. Someday, you will pay more of these taxes besides the sales tax.

Types of Governments and the Goods and Services They Provide

The federal government. The federal government passes and enforces laws that apply to everyone who lives in the United States. The United States president, vice president, members of the House of Representatives and the Senate, and nearly 3 million other people all work for the federal government. They work for the Defense Department, the Postal Service, the Peace Corps, the Veterans Administration, the Department of Agriculture, the federal court system, the Department of Transportation, the federal park system, the Federal Bureau of Investigation, the Central Intelligence Agency, and several other agencies. Each agency performs some job that can only be accomplished by the federal government.

The federal government does many things. It defends us from enemies, it runs the space program, it provides special aid to farmers, it runs the national park system, it maintains the federal highway system, it pays for scientific research, it provides electric power in some parts of the country, it provides income called *Social Security* to older people, and much more.

State governments. The United States is divided into 50 states. Each state has its own laws, but federal laws must be followed within each state. You have to follow the laws of your home state, and so do the people who visit or work in your state, but live in another state. The laws of the different states are pretty much alike. Most states are run by a governor and a lieutenant governor, and all states have a state legislature that makes laws. In all states except Nebraska, the state legislature is divided into two parts that are very much like the House of Representatives and the Senate in the federal government. More than 3 million people work for state governments.

State governments do things for the people of each state that the federal and local governments do not do. State governments support state college and university systems, run state parks, give financial aid to people who are out of work, and give money to cities and schools. They also build and maintain state hospitals, highways, and prisons.

All states have a state college or university system. These schools are supported, in part, by taxes that citizens and businesses pay to their state governments.

City and county governments. There are about 3,000 counties and 19,000 cities in the United States. Some cities are very small (some even have fewer than 100 residents) and some, such as New York City and Los Angeles, are very large. Counties are usually larger than cities and they usually contain several cities within their boundaries. There are also a few counties that contain exactly one city and no other land. New York City is so large that it contains five counties within its boundaries. Cities are usually governed by a mayor and a city council. In some New England states, members of the city council are called "selectmen." Counties are usually governed by a county board of commissioners. Counties typically do not have the equivalent to an elected mayor or governor. The county board of supervisors appoints an administrator who makes the day-to-day decisions about running the county.

Police protection is not really free, because everyone pays taxes to support the police department.

City and county governments do things that state and federal governments do not do. They pave and sweep the streets, and in the colder parts of the country, they remove snow from them. Many cities and counties run libraries, bus systems, parks, hospitals, and water systems. All city governments make some decisions about what can be built in them and where buildings can be located. Most cities, especially larger ones, are divided into areas, or zones, for different types of buildings. It is not by accident that houses are rarely located next to factories. Houses are built in areas that are designated or "zoned" for single family housing. Other zones that city councils can designate include heavy industrial, light industrial, commercial, and multifamily, or apartment, housing.

City and county police patrol the streets to prevent crime and to enforce traffic laws. City and county fire departments fight and prevent fires and monitor buildings for safety hazards. Cities and counties rarely charge people directly for the services they provide. People who live in the county or city, and the businesses that operate there, pay taxes. Those taxes are used to pay for the "free" city and county services.

School districts. There are nearly 15,000 public school districts in the United States. Some people attend private schools, but most U.S. citizens go to public schools from kindergarten through high school. One of the biggest differences between public and private schools is that students do not have to pay to attend a public school. You usually have to pay a fee, called tuition, to attend a private school. Public schools are not really free, because people and businesses pay taxes to the state and to the school district to support the schools. People pay these taxes whether or not they have children going to the public schools.

School districts are governed by a school board. The school board is elected by voters in the school district. The board appoints a superintendent of schools who, like the county administrator, makes the day-to-day decisions about running the school system.

Government in a Market Economy

When your family pays its taxes, it has less money left to spend on clothes, automobiles, or vacations. Governments spend the money they collect on such things as roads, schools, and space shuttles and they play an important role in the nation's **economy**. In a *market economy* such as we have in the United States, governments must buy the goods and services they use, in the same way you and your family buy the goods and services you use. Governments have to compete in the market economy for the goods and services they buy. When a government—even the federal government—buys things, it does not command businesses to sell to it. If a person or a private business is willing to pay more for a good or service than the government is willing to pay, then that person will buy the good or service and it will not be available to the government. Another name for all governments in the marketplace is the *public sector* and another name for families and businesses is the *private sector.*

Governments spend the money they collect in taxes on programs and projects that benefit the taxpayers and put money back into the economy. Governments also use the taxpayers' money to pay the salaries of 17 million government employees. In a way, you can think of government taxing and spending as a way to change the combination of goods and services that are bought and sold in the United States.

Sometimes, the government gives, or transfers, tax money back to the private sector. **Transfer payments** are not the same as government purchases of goods and services. With transfer payments, a government does not receive any labor or product in return for the payment it makes. Social Security, Aid to Families with Dependent Children, and unemployment compensation are all programs through which the public sector provides income to people who have retired or are unable to

Sometimes governments give special assistance to people who are having trouble. During drought conditions, the government might give aid to farmers who have lost their crop.

work. Governments also lend or give money to people, businesses, or regions of the country that need special help. This might include farmers, large businesses that are in danger of failing, states or counties where many people are unemployed, states or counties where there has been a disaster such as a hurricane or a tornado, or students who need loans to pay for college. When the federal government makes transfer payments to provide assistance in these special situations, the money is transferred to the state government, which in turn pays the money to individuals and businesses. U.S. citizens have come to expect the federal government to help people and parts of the economy that are having difficulty.

Candidates for public office will often promise better government services. But to provide these services, elected officials might have to raise taxes—a move that is likely to make them unpopular with voters.

How Much Government is Enough?

Since governments are involved in so many things that touch our lives every day, you might wonder if governments do too much, too little, or just enough for the people they serve. There is no right answer to this question.

One point of view—known as **laissez-faire**—says that governments should do only what is absolutely necessary to make certain that the country is not invaded by its enemies and that contracts and laws are enforced. According to this view, governments should provide only essential goods and services that cannot be furnished by the private sector. The opposite point of view is that the government should be more active. Government decisions about who to tax, what to tax, how much tax to charge, and how the government's money is spent can determine how much money consumers have to spend, whether many people will be unemployed, whether people will be opening new businesses, and many other things. As we shall see in later chapters, governments can sometimes be very active in the economy.

The role of the federal government in the United States economy is somewhere between these two extremes. The United States government now provides more goods and services than it did when your grandparents were your age. It costs a lot of money to run the new government programs, and taxes have gone up to pay for them. Generally, people do not want to give up large portions of their incomes in taxes, but a majority of voters want programs that require the government to spend more. So taxes usually increase from year to year.

In the rest of this book, we will look at different aspects of taxes and government spending in the United States. While everyone grumbles about taxes, few people grumble when they receive services from the government. It is important to look at taxes and government spending together. Are the benefits we receive from our governments worth as much as the taxes we pay for them? Each time we vote for public officials, we are giving our opinion about our governments' spending policies. If too many people are unhappy with a government's taxing and spending policy, its officials will not be reelected.

WHAT SHOULD A GOOD TAX SYSTEM BE LIKE?

When you buy something, like a shirt, it is yours. You own it. Owning a shirt means that you have the right to use that shirt. You may decide to share it with your brothers, sisters, or friends, but the shirt is yours. When you purchase that shirt, you prevent someone else from purchasing it. In a market economy, if many people want to purchase the same shirt, the seller may raise the price of the shirt and sell it to the person who is willing to pay the most. A seller who is not able to sell his or her supply of shirts might lower the price of the shirts until it is low enough that people will want to buy them. Things like shirts that are owned and sold by individuals and businesses in this way are called **market goods**.

There is another kind of good that is most often supplied by governments. This kind of good, called a **collective good**, is not like a market good for two important reasons. First, collective goods can be used by many people at the same time. Second, people usually do not pay to use collective goods. Any fee you might have to pay is much less than the cost of producing the collective good. Examples of collective goods are parks, schools, museums, police and fire protection, highway maintenance, and national defense.

Whether or not you take the bus to work, you are required to pay taxes so that bus service will be available to all citizens in your community.

When you use a city park, you do not pay a fee. The taxes your family and other families pay to the city cover the cost of operating the park. Even if you do not use the collective goods provided by your government—city, state, or federal—you are still required to pay the taxes to provide those services for all citizens.

Nearly every city has some kind of police force. When the police force patrols the streets, it does not charge your family for doing its work. The police look after your house and other houses in your neighborhood because your family and your friends' families pay their city taxes. If your house were robbed, the police officers would not check to see if your family had paid its taxes before they started to look for the thief. But a private protection service would not protect your home unless you had paid its bill.

Principles of Taxing and Spending

When any government decides to tax its citizens, it has to pass a law that describes the tax. This law says who will pay the tax, how much they will pay, when and where the tax must be paid, and what the punishment is if people do not pay their fair share. Congresspeople make rules about federal taxes, state legislators make rules about state taxes, county commissioners make rules about county taxes, and city council members make rules about city taxes.

People who make rules about taxation try to be certain that any taxes citizens have to pay are fair and that tax systems are efficient. Adam Smith (1723-1790), a Scottish economist, was the first person to describe how an ideal tax system should operate. In his famous book, *The Wealth of Nations*, which was published in 1776, Smith put forth several principles of taxation. In discussing taxes, economists still refer to the principles Smith described.

First, Smith said, people should contribute to the support of their government according to their *ability to pay*. The amount of taxes a person pays should be related to how much that person can afford. People with about the same amount of income or property should pay about the same amount of taxes. At the same time, Smith's *benefit principle* said that people who receive more benefits from the government should pay more taxes. Sometimes these two ideas conflict with each other because those who receive many government benefits may have little ability to pay taxes. Whether taxes should be based on benefits received or ability to pay is difficult to decide. We will return to this question in the next chapter.

Second, Smith wrote, each person should be able to easily compute the amount of taxes he or she owes. Citizens should be required to pay their taxes at a specific time and place. This principle means that the amount of taxes a citizen pays should be based on rates that are published and available to everyone.

Third, Smith said, people should be required to pay their taxes in a way that is convenient to them and at a time when they have the money to pay. For example, farmers should not be required to pay taxes on agricultural land until after the harvest, when they have been paid for the year's work.

Finally, Smith said, taxes should be as low as possible,

and the cost of collecting taxes should also be as low as possible. This final guideline means that there should be little money wasted in running the government. It also means that taxes should not be so high that people will not want to work. Smith believed—and many people still believe—that when taxes are too high, people will not work hard to produce goods and services, because they know that after they pay their taxes, there will be little money left for them to enjoy.

Adam Smith's tax principles, in summary, are that taxes should be charged, or levied, according to people's ability to pay; that tax payments should be related to the value of the benefits people receive; and that taxes should be levied according to law. They should be convenient to pay, as low as possible, and not expensive to collect.

Adam Smith described an ideal tax system in The Wealth of Nations. *While few people would call the U.S. tax system ideal, most would agree that the system plays a crucial role in keeping the economy and the government running efficiently.*

The United States tax system is, in large part, based on Smith's principles. Since the U.S. tax system has developed over more than 200 years, not every tax always follows all the principles.

The difference between Smith's ideal system and the United States tax system is related to economics, history, and politics. The amount of money that each kind of government needs to do its job changes as national and international economic and political situations change. If the United States were in an all-out war, the federal government would spend more money on defense than it does when the country is at peace. If there were an economic **recession** or **depression** and many people became unemployed, the federal and state governments would have to spend more to help people than they do when the economy is healthy.

Over time, taxes change. Sometimes the tax rates are increased or decreased. Sometimes new kinds of taxes are added. Sometimes, but not often, certain taxes are eliminated. Whenever these changes occur, they involve a lot of work and compromise for the people who guide our system of government taxing and spending—congresspeople, the president, state legislators, governors, county commissioners, and city council members. Each time they pass new tax laws, federal, state, and local legislators try to understand how the new tax will affect the economy, the people they represent, and the government they serve. Will poor people have to go hungry to pay the tax? Will the tax cause the economy to go into a depression? Will the tax raise enough money? Is it absolutely necessary for the government to have more money? These are some of the questions legislators

City council members must make difficult decisions about taxation.

have to answer. While people do not complain if their taxes are reduced, there is almost always opposition to a tax increase or to other changes in the tax system.

In the next chapter, we will look at some problems with Smith's ideal system and discuss how our tax system differs from Smith's basic principles.

3

HENNEPIN COUNTY MEDICAL CENTER
PARAMEDIC UNIT
ADVANCED LIFE SUPPORT
PARAMEDIC UNIT
POLICE
To Protect
To Serve
7647

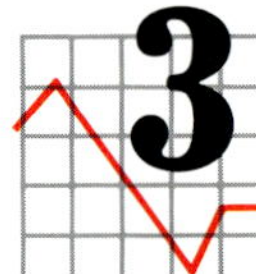

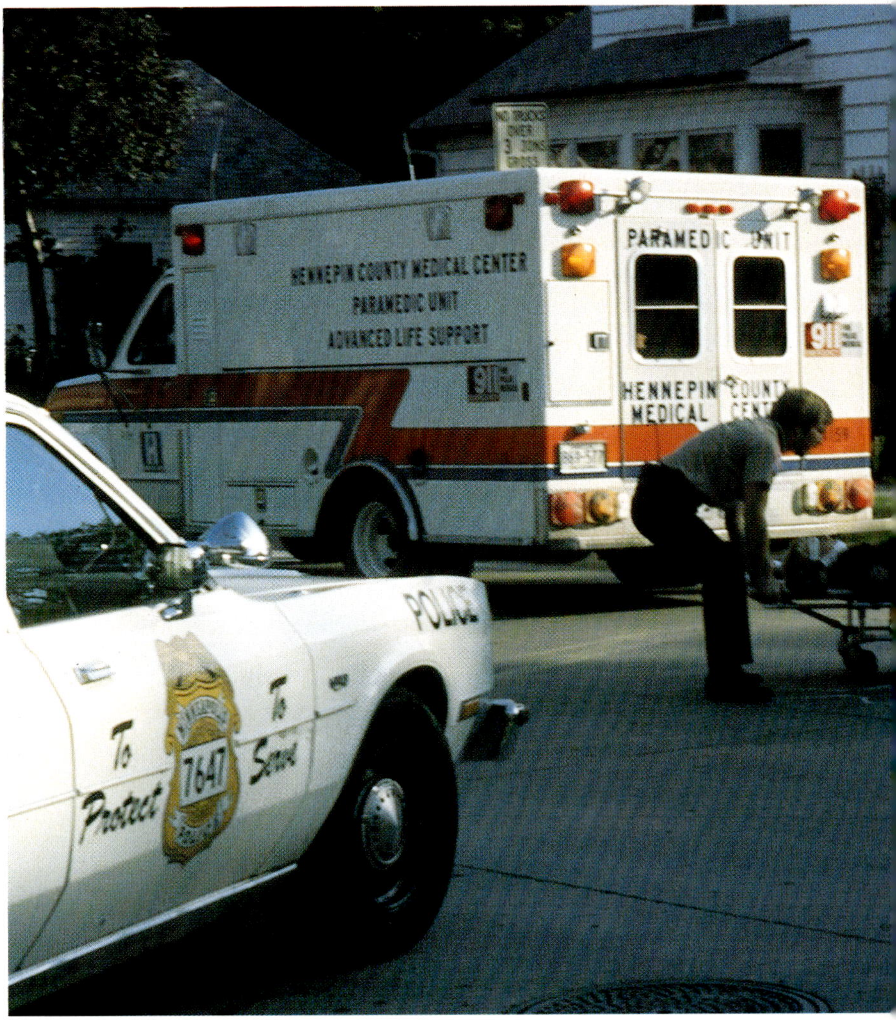

A CLOSER LOOK AT SMITH'S PRINCIPLES

Economists who study taxes and government spending agree that Adam Smith's principles describe taxation in an ideal world. Smith's first principle says that taxation should be based on the taxpayer's ability to pay and on the benefits the taxpayer receives from the government. But the first part of this principle often means the exact opposite of the second part. And it is often impossible to measure the value of the benefits a taxpayer receives from the government.

Measuring the Benefits We Get from Government Services

In our economic system, the taxes we pay are not always related to the benefits we receive. For example, people who receive transfer payments from the government usually do not pay taxes according to the amount of benefits they receive. Transfer payments are special payments that the government makes to people who are not able to work or to people who earn so little when they do work that they find it difficult to survive. Let's look at three important transfer payment programs that you may have heard about.

People who have lost their jobs and are looking for new ones may receive a transfer payment from their state government called *unemployment compensation.* The amount of unemployment compensation a person receives is based on the wage that the person earned before losing his or her job. The compensation is always much less than the person was earning on the job. Unemployment compensation is supposed to give some financial help while the unemployed person looks for a new job. Usually people can collect unemployment compensation for up to six months. In special circumstances, people may be allowed to collect unemployment compensation for up to a year. Special circumstances occur when there is a recession and many people are unemployed, or when a large firm closes and there are not other similar jobs in the area, so the people who were employed at that firm are not likely to find new jobs quickly.

Other people who may receive transfer payments are families with young children. Parents who have not

These people have lost their jobs and are filling out applications for unemployment compensation, a transfer payment that will provide some financial help while they look for new jobs.

been able to work and are not eligible to get unemployment compensation, or parents who work but earn very little money, may receive a transfer payment called _Aid to Families with Dependent Children_, or AFDC. Nearly all families that receive AFDC are headed by only one parent, usually the mother. AFDC payments are based on the size of the family and government estimates of living expenses for a family of that size. A family that receives AFDC payments gets very little money. The system is designed to give people who need it money that will help them pay rent and buy food, clothing, and health care. But it is not so much money that parents would choose to receive AFDC payments rather than work.

Social Security is a third important transfer payment that you may have heard about. When you start working, you will have to pay a special tax to the Social Security Administration. When you retire, or if you get sick or hurt and cannot work for more than six months, you will receive a Social Security payment from the federal government every month. If you have grandparents who are more than 65 years old, they probably receive some Social Security transfer payments.

Most people who receive transfer payments from the government need that money to survive. For them it is not "extra spending money." The benefits people get from their transfer payments are very large. But the ability of these people to pay taxes is very limited. If we were to tax people based on the benefits they receive from transfer payments, these people could not afford to pay their taxes. As a result, most transfer payments are not taxed at all. Most of the money the government uses to provide transfer payments comes from people who have the ability to pay taxes. But these people usually receive little, if any, benefit from transfer payments.

While it is easy to measure the value of some government services, such as transfer payments, it is extremely difficult to measure the value of other government services. Because there is no easy way to determine how much certain services are worth to the people who use them, governments often ignore the benefit principle. Instead, they tax everyone and give the service away at no charge.

It is impossible, for example, to measure the value of having a military service to defend the United States

Many people question the value of military spending. As long as the country is not at war, it is difficult to say what benefit people receive from the armed services.

from its enemies. Some people argue that money spent for weapons is money well spent. Other people argue that it is wasteful to spend money on weapons. As long as the United States is not invaded by a foreign country, it is impossible to say who is right. If the country were invaded, the military would defend everyone equally—even those people who thought spending money on military defense was useless—and the military would not charge anyone for its services. Everyone pays taxes to the federal government based on his or her ability to pay, and the benefits each person receives may be more or less than the amount that person has paid in taxes.

It is difficult to determine the value of a government benefit such as a paved street. If your street is paved, there might be less dirt in the air than there would be on a dirt road. Your house would not be as dirty and you would not have to repaint it as often as you might if you lived on an unpaved street. Your family's car would probably last longer, and it certainly wouldn't sink in the mud in front of your house after it rained. When you were ready to move, your parents would probably be able to sell the house for more money than they could if the house were on an unpaved street. Even though most people would agree that there are benefits a homeowner receives from living on a paved street, the value of many of these benefits is difficult to measure.

In cases like street paving, it is possible to say who benefits from the government service but not how much

How much benefit do you get from a paved street? It is difficult to measure the benefits, but chances are, if you live on a paved street, you will pay higher taxes than someone who lives on an unpaved street.

the benefit is worth. In this case, governments will divide the cost of providing the service among the people who will receive some benefit from it. With street paving, costs are usually divided according to the amount of property a person owns along the street. People who live in a house with a front yard that is 100 feet wide will pay more taxes than the people on the same street in a house with a front yard that is only 50 feet wide. Governments assume that the people who live in the house with the wider yard will receive more benefits from living on a paved street than the people who live in the house with the narrower yard. In this case, the government also assumes that the people who live in the house with the wider yard also have a greater ability to pay for having the street paved. Neither of these assumptions is always correct.

Measuring Taxpayers' Ability to Pay

Every tax has two parts, its **base** and its **rate**. The base is what is taxed. In the United States and in many other countries, there are three different tax bases: income (what you earn), consumption (what you buy), and property (what you own). The tax rate describes how much—or what percentage—of the value of the base is taxed. To find out your tax bill, you multiply your tax base times your tax rate. When your income is taxed, you pay a share of the money you earn to the government. When your consumption is taxed, you pay a share of the money you spend to the government—usually as sales tax. When your property is taxed, you pay a part of the value of the things you own to the government.

The first part of Adam Smith's first principle of taxation is that citizens should contribute to the support of government according to their ability to pay. This principle is usually interpreted to mean that people who have higher incomes should have a larger tax bill and should spend a larger share of their income on taxes than should people with lower incomes.

Progressive, proportional, and *regressive,* are words that describe whether tax rates increase, stay the same, or decrease as a person's tax base or income increases.

Progressive taxes increase as the tax base becomes higher. **Income taxes** are an example of progressive taxes. In the United States, people with lower incomes pay taxes at a lower rate than do people with higher incomes. Suppose that you go to work and earn $30,000 a year, and your friend goes to work and earns $50,000 a year. Let's also suppose that the tax rate for people who earn $30,000 is 20 percent and the tax rate for people who earn $50,000 is 30 percent. This means that you will pay 20 percent of your income and your friend will pay 30 percent of his income to the federal and state governments. Your tax bill will be $6,000 per year and your friend's tax bill will be $15,000 per year. Your friend, who earns more than you do, has to pay taxes at a higher rate than you do. When people with more money pay a higher tax, the tax is called progressive.

Regressive taxes are taxes that take a smaller share of the tax base or income as the tax base or income increases. **Property taxes** are often regressive. Again, let's look at you and your friend. Suppose your house is worth $40,000 and your friend's house is worth $60,000. You and your friend live in different cities. In your city the tax rate is 130 mills. (A mill equals one tenth of a penny.) Your property tax bill will be $520 per year. Your friend lives in a city where the tax rate is only 100 mills. Because the tax base—the value of the property—is larger in your friend's city, his city can raise the money it needs with lower rates. Your friend's tax bill will be $600 per year. Even though you make less money and live in a less valuable house, you are taxed at a higher rate and you pay almost as much in property taxes as your friend does. You must also spend a bigger part of your income paying property taxes than your friend does. Property taxes are often considered to be regressive, because they frequently fall most heavily on lower-income people.

Proportional taxes are taxes that stay at a constant rate, or percentage, regardless of the size of the tax base. The **sales tax**—the tax you pay when you buy almost anything—is a proportional tax. Let's look at you and your friend once more. Suppose you spend $15,000 a year and your friend spends $20,000 a year buying things on which you have to pay sales tax. You both have to pay a five percent sales tax on the things you buy. You will pay $750 per year in sales tax, and your friend will pay $1,000 per year. Your friend will pay more taxes, but that is because he buys more things that are taxed than you do. Even though you buy less than your friend, you spend a larger share of your income on things that are taxed. You also spend a larger part of your income paying sales tax. For this reason, proportional taxes are considered to be somewhat regressive.

TAXES IN THE UNITED STATES

If you have a part-time job, you probably spend only a very small part of your income on taxes. But someday you may have to use between one-fourth and one-half of the money you earn to pay taxes to federal, state, and local governments.

Taxes are very different from the other things you spend your money on. When you spend your money to buy an apple, you can see, touch, smell, and taste the apple. When you spend your money to pay taxes, the money goes to buy government services that you cannot see, touch, smell,

4

or taste. But those services still help you enjoy your life and the world around you. You are not required by law to buy apples, bicycles, and other things that you enjoy, but you are required by law to pay your taxes. If you do not pay your taxes, you could go to jail.

As we discussed in the previous chapter, governments in the United States tax three things—what you earn, what you spend, and what you own. We also learned that there are two parts to a tax, its base and its rate. The base refers to what is taxed, and the rate describes how much of the value of the base is to be paid in taxes. To compute the amount of tax you actually owe, you multiply the tax base times the tax rate. If the tax base is your income, the tax rate is 15 percent, and you earn $30,000—then your tax bill is $4,500 ($30,000 x 0.15 = $4,500).

Taxes on What You Earn

The federal government raises more of its money from income taxes than from any other tax. Almost half of the money that the federal government receives and almost one-fourth of the income that state governments receive comes from taxes on the incomes of businesses and people. New York City is one of the few local governments that levy an income tax. The income tax that people pay is called "personal income tax" and the income tax that corporations pay is called "corporate income tax."

Considering how important income taxes are to the state and federal governments, it is surprising that the income tax is one of the newest taxes in the United

States. In 1913, the Sixteenth Amendment to the U.S. Constitution made it legal for the federal government to establish an income tax. In 1911, Wisconsin became the first state to have a state income tax. Now all states except Nevada, Washington, and Wyoming have some kind of income tax.

Corporate income taxes. A corporation is a company that has satisfied legal requirements in order to become "incorporated." When a business is not a corporation, the business does not pay corporate income taxes. Instead, the owners of the business pay personal income taxes on their share of the earnings of the business. Calculating income tax is very complicated for most corporations and it may keep accountants busy all year long.

Personal income taxes. Most of us would have a hard time saving enough money to pay our income taxes every year if we had to pay the whole bill at once. To make it easier for you to pay your income taxes, your employer deducts, or **withholds**, a portion of your taxes from each paycheck you receive. The company sends the money that it withholds from your paycheck to the federal and state governments for you. The money that the employer withholds is probably not equal to the amount of taxes that you have to pay. It is usually pretty close to the correct amount, but it could be too much or too little.

By April 15 of each year (or April 16 or 17, if April 15 falls on a weekend), your total federal and state income taxes for the previous year are due. Either you will owe money to the government, or the government will owe you money because you paid too much in income taxes during the year. When the government owes you money,

Students apply for summer jobs. Since most students don't earn a lot of money, these boys will not have to pay income taxes on the money they earn or will receive a large tax refund from the government.

it refunds all or part of the income taxes that your employer withheld from your paycheck. Computing your taxes and figuring out how much you owe the state and federal government or how much your refund will be takes some time.

If you work after school at a fast-food restaurant, your employer might withhold income taxes from your paycheck. Since you probably don't earn a lot of money at your part-time job, your taxes will be very small. When you file a tax return form, the government will refund part—or maybe all—of the money your employer withheld from your paychecks.

Social Security tax. The Social Security tax is a special kind of income tax that is collected by the Social Security Administration. The Social Security Administration is part of the federal government. In 1988 each person's share of the Social Security tax was 7.51 percent of the first $45,000 that he or she earned. Employers withhold the Social Security tax money from a person's paycheck along with his or her income taxes. Employers also pay the same amount—7.51 percent of the first $45,000 that each employee earns each year—to the Social Security Administration.

When you retire, if you are injured or sick and cannot work for more than six months, or if one of your parents dies before you are 18 years old, you may receive money from the Social Security Administration.

Taxes on What You Earn and Smith's Principles

Personal and corporate income taxes are progressive taxes, since the tax rates get higher when a person's or a company's income increases. However, the Social Security tax is regressive. People whose wages or salaries are less than $45,000 per year pay 7.51 percent of their income to the Social Security Administration. This comes out to $3,379.50 per year for people whose wages or salaries are exactly $45,000. But people who earn more than $45,000 per year do not pay 7.51 percent of their income in Social Security taxes—they never pay more than $3,379.50, no matter how much they earn. The more a person earns over $45,000, the smaller the Social Security tax becomes as a portion of his or her income. For that reason, the Social Security tax is considered to be a regressive tax.

Income and Social Security taxes are convenient to pay, since the relatively small amounts that are withheld from each paycheck may add up to enough to pay all or most of your taxes by the end of the year.

Taxes on What You Spend

There are two different kinds of taxes collected on the money you spend in the United States—sales taxes and **excise taxes**. Sales taxes are collected by state and local governments, and most excise taxes are collected by the federal government.

Sales taxes. The sales tax is the tax that you probably know the most about, since you have to pay a sales tax on all or most of the things you buy. Almost all sales taxes in the United States are collected by state governments, but a few cities also charge a sales tax. The sales tax is the most important tax for most state governments. About 35 cents of every dollar that state and local governments raise come from sales taxes.

Each state makes its own rules about the sales tax it charges. A few states—Delaware, Montana, New Hampshire, and Oregon—do not charge sales tax at all. Sales tax is charged only to the last buyer or "final consumer" of a product. A bicycle manufacturer, for example, would not pay a sales tax when it purchased the steel used to build bicycles. But the person who buys the bicycle would be required to pay a sales tax.

Some states charge sales taxes on all final products people buy. People whose incomes are low spend a larger share of their incomes than people whose incomes are high. People whose incomes are low therefore, will spend a larger share of their incomes on sales taxes than people whose incomes are high. This means that the sales tax is somewhat regressive. In order to make the sales tax less regressive, some states do not collect any sales tax on some goods and services that are considered to be necessities, such as food, clothing, prescription drugs, and medical care. These goods and services are **exempt** from the sales tax.

Excise taxes. Excise taxes are almost like sales taxes. The biggest difference is that, while sales taxes are collected on most things, except for exempt goods and services, excise taxes are charged only on specific goods and services, most of which are considered to be luxuries. Excise taxes are charged on tobacco, liquor, gasoline, telephone service, and some things that are **imported** into the United States from foreign countries.

State governments collect a sales tax on most products and services. But sometimes necessities like food are not taxed.

Taxes on What You Spend and Smith's Principles

Sales and excise taxes are proportional taxes because they are set at a fixed percentage of the value of the tax base. But these taxes are regressive when you compare them to income, since people who do not earn a lot of money spend a larger share of their income on taxes than do people who earn a lot of money. These taxes are easy to compute and easy to pay, since the rates generally are low. The cost of collecting them is also low.

Taxes on What You Own

Taxes on what you own are called property taxes. Local governments depend on property taxes for most of their money. Some state governments also raise small amounts of revenue, or income, using property taxes. The federal government does not levy any property taxes. If you ever own a house, you will have to pay property taxes on the house. If you rent an apartment, you will not be required to pay the property taxes directly, but the landlord will use part of your rent money to pay the property taxes due on the apartment building.

There are two kinds of property—*real property* and *personal property*. Real property is land and things that are built on and attached to the land, such as buildings. Personal property is everything else we own, including the furniture in our houses and the machinery found in factories. Most states charge property taxes only on real property.

Deciding what property to tax and how to value that property is a very complicated process. Each state has its own procedures.

Property Taxes and Smith's Principles

Many people consider property taxes to be the most regressive taxes of all, particularly for retired people. Retired people often have very low incomes. But if a retired person bought a house when he or she was working, that person would still have to pay high property taxes after retirement.

Other Revenue Sources for Governments

In addition to tax money, local governments receive transfer payments from state and federal governments. State governments also receive transfer payments from the federal government. Governments obtain some money by charging a fee to people who use certain government services, including the United States Postal Service, state and national parks, toll bridges, and toll roads. Governments also charge license fees (in order to obtain a driver's license, for example, you must pass a test and pay a fee), and they charge permit fees for using government or public property. The federal government and many state governments also sell books and pamphlets that they publish. Some state and local governments own and operate liquor stores, and some local governments own and operate water, gas, and electric utilities. People who live in those communities might pay utility bills to the city instead of to a private company. The largest share of government revenues, however, is from taxes.

In the next chapter, we will look at the ways governments spend the money they collect from taxpayers.

5

HOW GOVERNMENTS SPEND THEIR MONEY

If you get an allowance or you have a part-time job, you have learned that you do not earn enough to buy everything that you want. You can buy some things with the money you earn in one week, but you might have to save your money for several weeks, or even several months, to be able to buy other things. When you decide how much of your money to save, how much money to spend, and what to spend your money on, you are making a **budget**. A budget is a plan describing the amount of money you expect to receive in a week, month, or year, and how you expect to spend that money.

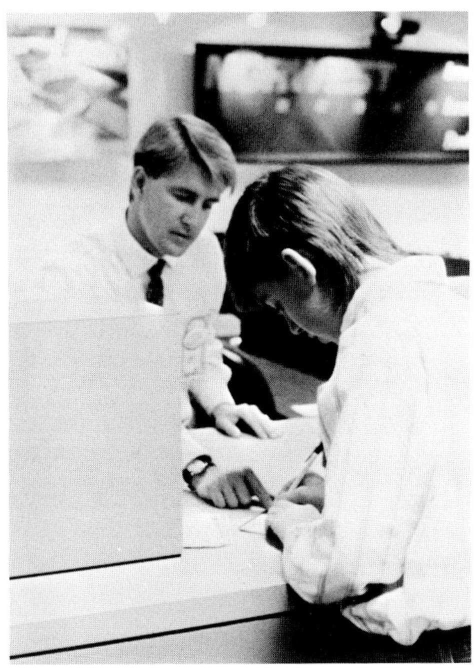

When you decide how much of your money to spend and how much to put into your savings account at the bank, you are making a budget.

Your parents do the same thing with the money that they earn. They decide how much of their money they can afford to spend on housing, food, clothing, transportation, entertainment, allowances for the children, and everything else. They must also decide how much money to put aside as savings for the future. If your family wants to buy a new car, for example, your parents might decide to see fewer movies or buy less clothing for a while in order to save money for the car. When your parents decide how to spend their money, they are making a budget. When you want your parents to buy something and they say, "We can't afford it," they are really saying, "It costs more than we have planned for in our budget."

Governments have budgets too. Just the way you often want more than you can afford, governments would often like to spend more than they can afford. If your parents do not have enough money to buy everything they want, there usually is not too much they can do about it except borrow money, work longer hours, or take a second job. If the federal government wants to spend more than it can afford, it can borrow money or increase taxes. Increasing taxes is something government officials do not like to do. If governments increase taxes too often or without good reason, taxpayers will vote the elected officials out of office as soon as possible. The federal government borrows money almost every year, but state and local governments do not usually borrow money.

How Governments Budget Their Money

The state and federal governments in the United States have three branches. Some local governments also have three parts or branches, but others have only two.

The first of the three branches is the *executive* branch. In the federal government, the executive is the president of the United States. Other governments also have executives. In state governments, the executive is the governor. In city governments, the executive is the mayor. In school districts, the executive is the superintendent of schools. In each kind of government, the executive branch is "in charge," but it has to follow the rules made by the second branch of government—the *legislative* branch.

In the federal government, the legislative branch is the Congress, which contains two chambers—the House of Representatives and the Senate. The legislative branch of your state government is its state legislature, which also has two chambers (except in Nebraska, where it has one). The legislative branch of city government is usually called the city council, and the legislative branch of a school district is usually called the board of education. The legislative branch of government is responsible for many things, including making laws, levying taxes, and approving budgets.

The third branch of government is the *judicial* branch. In this branch, judges make certain that the activities of the legislative and executive branches are legal and that laws are followed. The judicial branch is also responsible for determining whether or not people who have been accused of breaking the law are really guilty.

When it comes to making government budgets, the executive tells the legislative branch of government how much he or she wants to spend and what the money is to be spent on. The president, governor, or mayor does not actually prepare the budget him or herself. Many people who work for the government help prepare a part of the budget. In large cities and in the federal and state governments, some people spend all their time working on the budget all year long.

The executive and his or her staff begin by saying what they would like to spend money on and how much money will be needed for each project or program. The staff members then have to forecast how much money they think the government will have available to spend from tax money and other revenue. The larger the government, the more complicated this becomes and the more time it takes. If the executive wants to spend more money than will be available, he or she must

Long before heavy machinery tears up your street, your city council has approved a budget that includes money for road repair.

either cut some projects from the budget or ask the legislative branch to raise taxes. The executive can also ask the legislative branch to reduce taxes if the government thinks it will have more money than it needs.

Once a year (or once every two years in most state governments), the executive presents his or her proposed budget to the legislative branch of the government. The legislators (or city council or school board members) go over the budget carefully, and often they make changes if they think the executive is planning to spend too much or too little money. They also may decide to increase taxes if they think the government needs to have more money. They might decide to increase the tax *rate* in order to raise this money, or they might decide to change the tax *base* by levying a new tax, such as a sales tax on food.

Once the legislative branch passes a budget, it sends the budget back to the executive for his or her approval. Only then does the budget actually become law. If the new budget requires changes in the tax rate or base, these changes might not take place for several months. In the federal government, it takes six to nine months from the time the president proposes a budget until the Congress passes it and sends it back to the president for approval. In state governments, it takes three to five months from the time the governor proposes a budget until the state legislature sends the budget back to the governor for his or her signature.

How Governments Spend Their Money

When your parents make their budget, or financial plan, for the year, they have to be careful that they do not spend more money than they will earn. The federal government is the one government that is allowed to spend more money than it receives each year. When a government spends more than it has collected in taxes during the year, it has a **deficit**.

Between 1929 and 1988, the federal government had a deficit in all but eight years. In 1979 the federal government deficit was $72, and in 1988 it was $630, for each person who lived in the United States. The deficit is the amount of money the government has to borrow each year. The total amount of money the government has borrowed over the years, minus the amount of money it has repaid, is the government **debt**. The federal government was borrowing more and more money each year between 1979 and 1988, so the total amount of the

Some of the money that the federal government collects goes to help farmers improve crops and growing methods (above). Some money is transferred to state governments where it might be spent on education (right).

federal government's debt grew from $3,700 to $11,700 per person. In the next chapter we will take a closer look at the federal government deficit.

In 1988, the federal government spent about $2,600 for each person who lived in the United States. This money was spent to pay the salaries of everyone who worked for the federal government, to buy weapons and other things the federal government needed, to make transfer payments to state and local governments, and to pay **interest** on the federal debt. Another $1,700 per person was spent on transfer payments from the Social Security Administration, but these expenditures were supported by special taxes.

The biggest share of the federal government's money is spent on national defense. More than 28 cents of every dollar the federal government spent in 1988 went to defense and international relations. The money was used to pay the salaries of people in the army, navy, marine corps, air force, and coast guard. It also paid for new airplanes and missiles, and it ran army and navy bases all over the world.

About 10 cents of every dollar the federal government spent in 1988 was transferred to state and local governments. This money went to programs such as unemployment compensation and AFDC, highways, education, and other special projects the federal and state governments work on together. That is about $440 for each person living in the United States.

The rest of the money the federal government spent went to pay interest on the national debt, maintain natural resources such as the national park system, pay the salaries of the people who work for the federal

Twenty-eight cents of every dollar that the federal government spends goes to the military: the army, the navy, the marine corps, the air force, and the coast guard.

government, and to support many other programs like crop subsidies for farmers and scientific research.

State and local governments. In 1988, state and local governments spent about $2,700 for every person who lived in the United States. That total includes the $440 per person that state and local governments received from the federal government.

State and local governments spend more money on education than on anything else. More than 34 cents of every dollar that state and local governments spent in 1988 went to public education. That is about $1,000 each for you, your parents, and everyone else that you know. If we divide that money among people who attend a public school, it is over $3,000 per student. This money goes to pay teachers' salaries, buy books, heat and maintain schools, operate the school bus system, and pay all the other costs of running more than 14,800 school systems in the United States.

The next largest expenditure made by state and local governments goes to help people who are having some financial difficulty. Nearly 13 cents of every dollar that state governments spent in 1988 went to some kind of public welfare such as unemployment compensation and ADFC. That was more than $335 for every person living in the United States in 1988. Some states run public welfare programs themselves and others transfer money to counties, which distribute these funds.

About eight cents of every dollar that state and local governments spent in 1988 was for highways. That was about $200 for each person in the United States.

Almost half of the money state and local governments spent in 1988—nearly 45 cents out of every dollar—was spent on libraries, public hospitals, transportation, housing and community development, public water and

State and local governments almost never have deficits. These governments can only borrow money for long-term building projects like bridges and roads.

sewer systems, police and fire protection, and a number of other services.

Laws in many states require state and local governments to have "balanced budgets" every year. That means that unlike the federal government, state and local governments cannot plan to have deficits. If a government accidentally has a deficit one year, it must repay it quickly. State and local governments are only allowed to borrow money to fund certain projects, such as buildings and bridges that will last a long time. The governments generally do not have enough money to pay for these projects all at once and it is thought that the people who will use these projects in the future should pay part of the cost.

Nearly all state and local governments spend less money than they raise each year in taxes and payments from other governments. When governments spend less than they collect, they have a surplus. When state and local governments have a surplus, legislators try to cut taxes the following year.

Your state and local governments have annual financial reports, and you can get copies of them if you would like to learn more about how these governments spend their money.

Governments spend a lot of money, nearly all of which is supposed to make our lives better. That is what we will look at in the next chapters—can government spending improve our lives? But first we must ask, are our governments spending too much?

THE FEDERAL GOVERNMENT DEFICIT

In the last chapter, we talked about the federal government deficit. In 1988, the federal government collected $909 billion in taxes and spent $1,064 billion. Since the government spent more than it took in, it had to borrow the difference from people, companies, and foreign countries. In 1988 the federal government borrowed $155 billion—nearly $630 for each person who lived in the United States.

But 1988 was not the first time the federal government borrowed money. The federal government has been borrowing money, repaying some, and borrowing more throughout the history of the United States. The amount

of money the federal government borrowed began to increase steadily beginning in the 1940s. Even after we subtract the money that the federal government had repaid, it still owed $2,601 billion—or $2.6 trillion—at the end of 1988. This is nearly $11,700 for each person who was living in the United States in 1988.

$2,601 billion is a lot more money than the federal government can raise in taxes! If the government were to collect taxes at the same rate it did in 1988, it would have to collect taxes and not spend any money for two years and seven months in order to pay back its entire debt. No one would seriously consider having the government save all of our taxes for nearly three years. If the federal government stopped spending, all the people the government employs would lose their jobs, and so would many people who work for companies that sell things to the government. With so many people unemployed, the government would have a very hard time collecting taxes!

Does the fact that the government owes so much money mean that it is broke? Do we need to worry about the federal deficit? Can the federal government keep on borrowing money?

In order to answer these questions, you need to learn another economics term: **gross national product**. Gross national product, which is often just called GNP, is the total value of the goods and services that everyone in the country has produced in a year. Nearly every country in the world calculates its own GNP. We often compare the GNP per person in different countries. In general, the higher the per-person GNP in a country, the more goods and services are available in the economy.

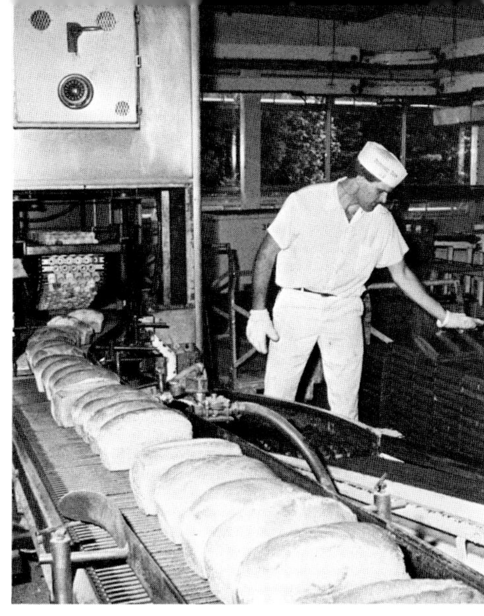

The total value of all the goods and services that a country produces in a year is called its gross national product, or GNP.

The GNP per person in the United States is one of the highest in the world.

GNP measures only what has been produced in a year. It does not measure the value of what has been produced in the past that we still use. The value of all these things that were produced in the past and which we still use, minus any money that we still owe on them, is our **national wealth**. The national wealth in the United States is also very high.

To understand how big the annual deficit and the total debt really are, you need to compare them to something. Since the federal government affects all of us, we need to compare the deficit to something, like GNP, which also affects everyone. In 1988, GNP was $4,780 billion, or $19,500 for every person in the United States. The deficit was about $630 per person. Put that way, the deficit does not seem so big. If you earned $19,500 a year and you had to borrow $630, probably no one would say you could not manage your money—unless you had to borrow $630 *every* year and never paid it back.

The U.S. government has *always* paid its debts on time. Often it has made the payment on its debt by borrowing more money. This borrowing can have both good and bad effects on the economy, as we shall see.

Now we can say two important things about the federal government's deficit: It is very large when you just look at the number of dollars involved; it is not very large at all when you compare it to GNP and national wealth.

Is the Federal Government Broke?

The answer to this question is no. The government is able to borrow so much money because the U.S. economy is a healthy economy and is expected to remain healthy. The money the federal government has borrowed has been used to build power plants and roads, to fund schools and colleges, to buy land for national parks, and to pay for scientific research. All these things provide jobs, help us manufacture new goods, and make it possible for the United States to continue to grow. Countries with healthy economies are able to pay back the money they have borrowed because their economies grow and generate more money than the country originally borrowed.

Governments usually borrow money for a specific purpose, and they spend the money as soon as they receive it. When the borrowed money is spent to build highways, power plants, or spacecraft, it ends up in people's paychecks and puts income back into the economy. This income is then taxed. One way of looking at government debt, then, is that it causes the economy to produce fewer market goods and more collective goods.

When governments spend money to build a road, a power plant, or even a museum (above), more people have jobs and more people pay taxes.

Do We Need to Worry about the Deficit?

The answer to this question is maybe. Borrowing money makes most of us nervous. The United States has always been able to borrow money, but what if our growth stops and we cannot pay our debts and cannot borrow any more money?

When the federal government—or anyone else—borrows money, it pays back the money, plus some more money called *interest.* The lender lets someone borrow money in order to earn interest on the loan. If you borrow money from your parents or your brothers or sisters, they probably will not charge you interest. But if you or your parents borrow money from a bank, the bank will charge interest on the loan.

The United States has always paid the interest on its debt on time. As long as the United States government is able to pay the interest on its debt, and as long as it is able to repay the amounts it has borrowed when the loans are due, it will continue to be able to borrow money.

One problem with a large government debt is that as the debt gets larger and larger, more and more of our tax dollars are used to pay the interest on our debt. So much money goes to pay interest that there is less money available for national parks, federal prisons, or airplanes for the army.

For a long time, economists have said that there is no need to worry about the federal government debt because "we owe it to ourselves." When the government issues **bonds** in order to borrow money, the bonds are often owned by citizens of the United States.

If you ever received a United States bond as a gift, it was because someone—perhaps a grandparent—made a loan to the United States government for you. You will receive the amount of money your grandparent lent the government, plus interest on the loan, when the bond matures, which is a fancy way of saying when the loan is due.

People and businesses to whom the federal government owes money think of their government bonds as part of their wealth. If you own any U.S. government savings bonds, you know that someday you will receive some money from the federal government. But your savings bonds are also part of the federal government's debt.

Between 1977 and 1988, the federal government deficit increased by more than three times. It grew from $54 billion in 1977 to nearly $155 billion in 1988. In 1986, it was $221 billion. During the same period, GNP increased by only two and a half times. GNP grew from $1,933 billion in 1977 to $4,780 in 1988. The deficit was growing faster than the value of goods and services we were producing. As the government was borrowing more and more, people, banks, and companies in the United States were willing to lend the government money only if the government would pay a higher interest rate than it had before. As interest rates were rising, people, banks, and companies in foreign countries, particularly Japan and West Germany, began to buy a larger and larger share

A government savings bond. The bond represents a debt owed by the federal government. But to the bondholder, who will earn interest on the loan, it also represents wealth.

of U.S. government bonds. In 1977, foreigners lent the U.S. government and businesses $37 billion. In 1987, they lent $106 billion.

Because a large share of the U.S. debt is owed to investors in other countries, we don't really owe our debt "to ourselves" anymore. Since more and more United States bonds are owned by foreigners, each year a larger and larger share of our GNP is used to pay interest to foreigners. As a result, each year a smaller share of our GNP is available for people in the United States.

Can the Federal Government Keep Increasing the Deficit?

The basic answer to this question is yes, but not without some limits. There are some things that stop the government from borrowing money to pay for everything and keep the debt from growing too large.

First, the United States's **credit** has always been very good, but if the government issued too many bonds, its credit might no longer be considered good. We cannot say how much debt is "too much," but if people stopped buying U.S. government bonds, or the value of GNP fell, it would indicate that the government had issued too much debt. These would be signs that the United States might not be able to pay the interest on its debt. If the United States had bad credit, it would have to pay very high interest rates in order to keep borrowing, or show the rest of the world that it could pay its debts by raising taxes, laying off government workers, or spending less money for things like highways.

Second, the federal debt is not scheduled to mature,

or become due, all at one time. The bonds that the government issues mature on many different dates. Some mature next week, others will mature in 30 years, and still others will mature somewhere in between. Whenever bondholders are paid, they spend the money they receive on goods, services, and taxes. This gives income back to the economy.

A third safeguard that prevents the public debt from growing without limit is that the U.S. economy continues to grow. People's incomes increase nearly every year. This means that the federal government has a larger pool of income to tax, and it can use this money to pay the interest on its debt as well as to pay off some of the debt as it becomes due.

A fourth factor that prevents the federal government's debt from increasing is that, since 1986, it has been against the law for the deficit to get larger. In 1986, Congress passed the Gramm-Rudman-Hollings Act. This law said that the federal deficit had to get smaller by certain amounts each year until the federal government's budget was balanced in 1993. The Act also said that if Congress could not decide which of its programs were to be cut, all programs, except Social Security, had to be cut to reduce the deficit. The deficit has gotten smaller in the late 1980s.

Almost more important than the size of the deficit is how the deficit affects the U.S. economy, and what the borrowed money is spent on. That is the topic we turn to next. How can government spending and borrowing affect the level of GNP?

CAN GOVERNMENT SPENDING MAKE A DIFFERENCE?

If you have ever asked your parents if you could borrow money from them, they almost certainly asked you what you were going to do with the money. You may have discovered that your parents were more willing to lend you money if you were going to use it to buy a book than if you were going to use it to go to a roller-skating party. It makes more sense to spend borrowed money on something that will last, than to spend it on something that gets used up right away. When you have to pay back the money you have borrowed, you will still have the book, but you might not even remember the roller-skating party.

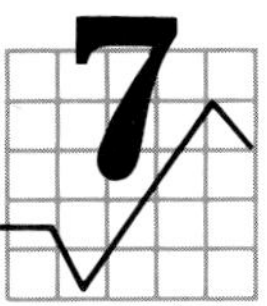

FOR DEFENSE
BUY
UNITED
STATES
SAVINGS
BONDS
ON SALE AT YOUR ... BANK

7

Highways make it easier for people to get to work and for businesses to manufacture and deliver goods and services. People are likely to approve of deficit spending for projects like highways that improve their lives and help the economy grow.

When the government borrows money, it commits our *future* taxes to repay debt. Taxpayers are more likely to approve of deficit spending when the money is spent on roads, schools, and scientific research—things that may make it easier to pay future taxes—than when the money is spent on transfer payments and defensive weapons—things that will not add as much to the economy's ability to produce new goods and services. Roads, schools, and scientific research all may make it easier for us to pay taxes in the future, because each of those things might make it possible for companies to produce more goods and services. If companies produce more, more people will have jobs and more people will be paying taxes.

What is Fiscal Policy?

Fiscal policy is a tool that the federal government uses to keep unemployment and **inflation** as low as possible. Inflation means that prices of the things you want to buy keep rising.

Fiscal policy describes the way the federal government taxes and spends. Choosing to have a deficit in order to accomplish its goals is an example of how the federal government uses fiscal policy.

Until some time after 1936, most economists thought that one of the best things governments could do for their citizens was to keep taxes low and keep the budgets balanced. At that time, the whole world was in the middle of the Great Depression that had begun in 1929.

In a depression, companies are unable to sell what they produce, so they reduce the number of people who work for them. During the depression of the 1930s, for every 100 adults who wanted to work, 20 were not able to find jobs. In 1936, an English economist named John Maynard Keynes published a book called *The General Theory of Employment, Interest, and Money.* This

Unemployed men wait for a meal at a soup kitchen during the Great Depression of the 1930s. John Maynard Keynes suggested that the government spend its way out of the depression.

book, which many economists think is the most important economics book of the 20th century, suggested that the federal government could *spend* a country out of the depression by deliberately having a deficit. The idea was that if the government spent money, more people would be employed and then they would spend more money. That would encourage businesses to expand, build more factories, and order new equipment. That would put even more people to work, and so on.

The federal government under President Franklin D. Roosevelt began to take on small deficits in the middle 1930s. The Great Depression lasted until the 1940s when government spending rose rapidly and the government took on the big deficits that were necessary to pay for weapons and supplies during World War II. Under President Roosevelt, the federal government took a much more active role in running the economy than it ever had before. The federal government has continued to remain active.

Franklin D. Roosevelt served as president during the Great Depression, a time of economic despair, and during World War II, a time of economic recovery.

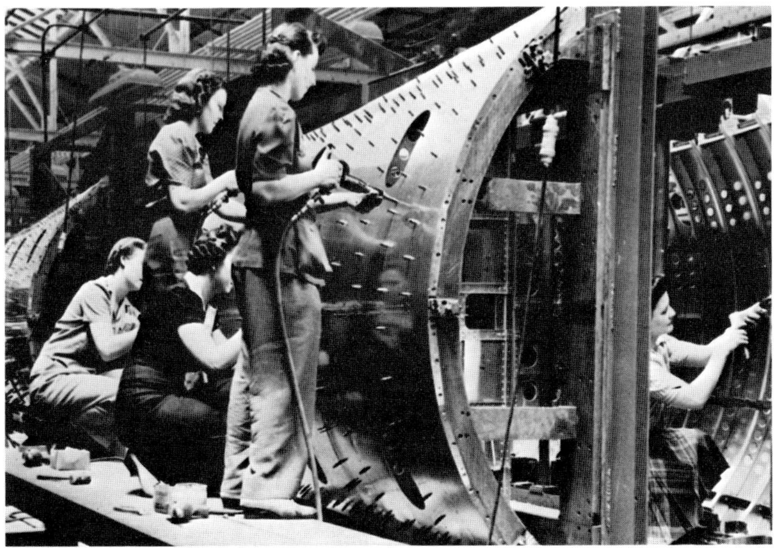

Under Roosevelt, the government began to take on small deficits. It borrowed money and put people to work on projects such as the Civilian Conservation Corps (above).

World War II brought about bigger deficits. The government needed to borrow money to pay for weapons and military supplies. Military spending bolstered the economy and put thousands of people to work in the war industries.

How Does Fiscal Policy Work?

This question requires a rather complicated answer. In the last chapter, gross national product, or GNP, was defined as "the total value of the goods and service that everyone has produced in a year." There are two ways to compute GNP: one is to add up the value of what everyone in the country receives, and the other is to add up the value of what everyone spends. You get the same value of GNP no matter which way you compute it.

There are four general areas of spending—consumption, investment, government spending, and net exports.

Consumption is the spending done by all the people in the economy. It is the sum of all of our spending on food, clothing, toys, refrigerators, and everything else we buy. Consumption does not include anything that a business purchases and resells to another business. When your mother buys a loaf of bread at the grocery store, the amount she spends on the bread is part of our nation's consumption for the year. That amount gets added into GNP. When a miller buys wheat from a farmer, a baker buys flour from a miller, or a grocer buys bread from a baker, these purchases are not part of consumption and do not get added into GNP.

Investment is what businesses produce, but do not sell to people. Investment includes the value of buildings, machinery, and things on store shelves at the end of the year that have not been sold.

Government spending is the money that all governments—federal, state, and local—spend to pay employees and to buy things such as paper clips, fire engines, and bombers.

Net exports is the difference between the amount

the United States sells to people and businesses in foreign countries and the amount the U.S. buys from people and businesses in foreign countries. Each year between 1983 and 1987, the United States bought, or imported, more goods from foreign countries than it was able to sell, or export, to them. When imports are bigger than exports, GNP is reduced. No country likes to import more than it exports for very long.

The federal government uses fiscal policy—the way it taxes people and businesses and the way it spends money—to influence consumption, investment, and net exports. For example, the more money people have, the more they will be able to spend. So the government can influence consumption by changing the amount of money people have to spend. If people have more money, the government cannot force people to spend it, but they will usually spend at least part of it.

Politicians know that cutting taxes will make them popular with voters. But tax cuts can also help the economy. If people have more money to spend, they will probably spend it.

The government can change the amount of money people have in two ways. It can change the amount of taxes people have to pay, and it can change the amount of money it spends. If the federal government increases taxes, GNP can be expected to fall or to increase more slowly than it has in the past, since people will have less money to spend. If the government increases its spending, GNP will rise, since people will have more money to spend. Suppose the government increases spending by a billion dollars. GNP will rise as a result. But it will rise by a lot more if the spending is financed with a deficit than it will if the extra spending is financed by a billion dollars of new taxes.

The government can encourage or discourage businesses from buying new buildings and machinery by the way it taxes or does not tax these expenditures. The government can also make it more or less attractive for foreigners to sell things in the United States by increasing or decreasing taxes on imported goods.

Does Fiscal Policy Really Work?

In one sense, every time the president proposes a budget to Congress, and Congress passes a budget, the federal government is using fiscal policy. If the president and Congress decide that the economy needs to grow, and they decide to increase government spending and decrease taxes at the same time, that is also fiscal policy.

One of the earliest and most important examples of fiscal policy working very well occurred in 1963. Then President John F. Kennedy enacted a tax cut and did not decrease government spending. There had been

When the John F. Kennedy administration cut taxes, the economy grew quickly.

more unemployment than the government wanted for some time. The tax cut gave people more money to spend, and when they spent more money, the economy grew much more quickly than it had for several years.

In the early 1980s, President Ronald Reagan also tried to make the economy grow. He asked Congress to make large tax cuts in 1982 and 1983. He believed that if taxes were cut, people would have more money to spend and they would spend it—all of which would make the economy grow. At the same time, he asked Congress to increase spending on defense. President Reagan and his advisors hoped that the economy would grow rapidly because of the tax cut. They hoped that the growth would be great enough to reduce the deficit. Even though the tax cut meant that people were paying taxes at lower rates, the president reasoned, it also meant more people would be employed and able to pay taxes. Even more importantly, people would be paying taxes on higher

President Reagan increased defense spending and cut taxes, thinking that the economy would grow as a result. GNP grew, but it couldn't keep pace with the federal deficit, which ballooned from $54 billion in 1977 to $155 billion in 1988.

incomes. The economy grew steadily following the tax cut, but so did the deficit.

There are many reasons why President Reagan's tax plan did not work. Economists who opposed the plan felt that since the tax cut was so large, and the president was determined to spend so much on defense, there was no way that tax revenues could ever grow enough to reduce the deficit. As the deficit grew larger each year, Congress decided it would force the deficit to get smaller by enacting the Gramm-Rudman-Hollings Act. This act states the amount by which the deficit must shrink each year.

One of the things we have learned since President Kennedy first proposed a tax cut to stimulate the economy is that if the economy is doing well and we try to make it grow, this will cause inflation, or rising prices.

Suppose the federal government tried to stimulate the economy by cutting taxes and increasing spending. Businesses would have more money to expand and they would build new plants, buy new equipment, and hire new workers. With so many businesses expanding, workers, materials, and equipment would be in great demand. To get the laborers and supplies they needed, the companies might have to pay more than ever before. If businesses have to pay more for the things they need, they will also raise the prices of the things they sell to make up the difference. When prices go up, people demand higher wages. Prices and wages keep on rising—first one and then the other—in a cycle of inflation.

From the late 1960s to the early 1980s, there was more inflation in the economy than most people agreed was acceptable. Much of that inflation began when President Lyndon Johnson increased the federal government deficit to finance the war in Vietnam and to conduct a special program called "The War on Poverty." Both wars were very expensive, and at the time, there was so little unemployment in the economy that inflation began to increase.

After Lyndon Johnson left office, presidents Nixon, Ford, and Carter had a different problem than any presidents before them ever had. When those men were president, there was more inflation *and* more unemployment than most people wanted. Between 1970 and 1980, the prices of most of the things we buy more than doubled. This means you needed $2.12 in 1980 to buy the same things you could have bought for $1.00 in 1970. These presidents recognized that reducing inflation by increasing taxes or decreasing government spending would increase unemployment. But reducing unemployment by increasing government spending or reducing taxes would increase inflation.

Have economists learned anything since the federal government first began to think seriously about fiscal policy in the late 1930s? Yes, of course. Economists have learned that fiscal policy is a very powerful tool that must be used carefully.

Government decisions about taxing and spending—from federal fiscal policy to the town budget—affect our lives in many ways. Some of these effects are easy to see, and some are not as easy to see. When your city spends money to repair a road, it is easy to see how the citizens will benefit from the tax dollars they have spent. But why pay to support the city bus system if you have your own car? Why pay money to support the military if the country isn't at war? Even though we may not use the government services we pay for right now, just knowing that these services will be available if we need them is important to most people. It is very easy to complain that taxes are too high. Many people do. At the same time, it is important to remember that governments provide services that we all use. The next time you pay sales tax at the store, think about all the services you receive from your federal, state, and local governments and the many ways in which they benefit your life.

bond—A certificate representing a debt owed by a corporation or a government.

budget—The income and spending plans of a person, family, business, or government for some future time period, such as a year

collective good—A good that is not owned by one individual and can be used by more than one person at a time. Collective goods are usually provided by governments.

consumption—The spending done by all the people in the economy during a specific time period, like a year.

credit—The extent to which a person, company, or government can borrow money. The amount of credit available is based on the borrower's income, financial stability, and previous record of repaying loans.

debt—The total amount of money the government has borrowed over the years, minus the amount of money it has repaid

deficit—The amount of money the government has to borrow each year

depression—An extended slump in business activity

economy—The system of the production and distribution of goods and services in a country, area, or time period

excise tax—A tax on the sale of particular goods, such as cigarettes, liquor, and gasoline

exempt—Not taxed

exports—Goods or services that are produced in the United States and sold in a foreign country

fiscal policy—The federal government's spending and taxing policy, which is designed to keep everyone employed and prices stable

gross national product—The value of goods and services produced in a country in a year.

interest—The cost of borrowed money

import—Goods or services that are produced in a foreign country and sold in the United States

income tax—A tax on the income of people (personal income tax) or corporations (corporate income tax)

inflation—A general increase in the level of prices

investment—What businesses produce, but do not sell to people. Investment includes the value of buildings, machinery, and things on store shelves at the end of the year that have not been sold.

laissez faire—A policy that government should not interfere with the economy

market goods—Goods and services that can be purchased and owned by individuals and businesses

national wealth—The value of all the things that were produced in the past, which we still use

progressive tax—A tax that increases as the tax base or income increases

property tax—A tax on the value of land and buildings. In some states there are property taxes on other things that people and businesses own.

proportional tax—A tax that stays at a constant share of the tax base or income as the tax base or income increases

recession—A period of decreased business activity
regressive tax—A tax that takes a smaller share of the tax base or income as the tax base or income increases

sales tax—A tax on the selling price of a good
Social Security—A federal program that taxes the first $45,000 of nearly everyone's income. When people retire or if they become disabled, they can collect Social Security benefits.

taxation—A system of raising money to finance government services and activities
tax base—The thing that is taxed. The tax bases used in the United States are consumption, property, and income.
tax rate—The rate, or percentage, at which something is taxed. Sales, for instance, might be taxed at a rate of five percent of the price of the item being purchased.
transfer payments—Payments made by governments, which do not pay for goods and services. Examples of transfer payments are unemployment compensation, Social Security, and AFDC.

withholding—A portion of employees' incomes that employers withhold, or do not pay, to the employees. The employers send this money to the government as tax payments. The amounts withheld are usually close to, but not exactly equal to, the amount the employee owes the government.

Aid to Families with
   Dependent Children
   (ADFC), 16, 31

budgeting, 49-54
bonds, 66-68

city government (see local
   government)
collective goods, 22
consumption, 76
corporate income taxes, 41
county government (see local
   government)

debt, 54; of federal
   government, 62-69
defense spending, 32-33, 56,
   79-80
deficit, 54; of state and local
   governments, 59; of federal
   government, 60-69

economic growth, 64, 68, 72,
   78-81
excise tax, 45

federal government, 11-12;
   debt, 62-69; defense
   spending, 32-33, 56, 79-80;
   deficit, 60-69; fiscal policy,
   72-82; government bonds,
   66-67, 68; spending, 56-57
fiscal policy, 72-82
foreign debt, 67-68

*(The) General Theory of
   Employment, Interest, and
   Money*, 73-74
government, branches, 51-54;
   budgeting, 51-54; revenue
   (non-tax-generated), 10, 47;
   services, 8-19, 29-35, 49-59;
   spending, 49-59, 71-82
Gramm-Rudman-Hollings
   Act, 69, 80
Great Depression, 73-74
gross national product
   (GNP), 62-64, 76-78

income taxes, 36, 40-42
inflation, 72, 81-82
interest, 65-66
interest rates, 67
investment, 76

Johnson, Lyndon, 81

Kennedy, John F., 78-79
Keynes, John Maynard, 73-74

laissez-faire, 18
local government, 13-15;
   spending of, 57-59

market economy, 16, 21
market goods, 22

national wealth, 63, 64
net exports, 76-77

personal income taxes, 41-42
private sector, 8, 16
progressive taxes, 36, 43
property taxes, 36, 46-47
proportional taxes, 37, 45

Reagan, Ronald, 79-80
regressive taxes, 36-37, 43,
    45, 46-47
Roosevelt, Franklin D., 74

sales taxes, 7, 37, 44-45
school districts, 15
Smith, Adam: principles of
    taxation, 23-25, 29-37, 43,
    45-46, 46-47
Social Security Administration:
    benefit payments, 16, 32,
    43; taxes, 32, 42-43
state government, 12;
    spending of, 57-59

taxation, 7-11, 23-27, 35-37,
    38-47
tax bases, 35-37, 40-46
tax rates, 35-37, 40
transfer payments, 16-17,
    30-32, 58

unemployment, 73, 78, 81-82
unemployment compensation,
    16, 30

Vietnam War, 81

"War on Poverty," 81
withholding, 41, 42, 43
Wealth of Nations, 24-25
World War II, 74

ACKNOWLEDGMENTS

Photographs and illustrations in this book are used courtesy of:
Brian Rose/Metropolitan Museum of Art, p. 2; Karen Sirvaitis,
pp. 6, 13, 45, 58, 65, 72, 77; U.S. Post Office, p. 9; Yellowstone
National Park, p. 10; Minneapolis Police Department, pp. 14, 28,
88; U.S. Department of Agriculture, pp. 17, 55 (top); League of
Women Voters of Minnesota, 18; Minneapolis Fire Department,
p. 20; Metropolitan Transit Commission, p. 22; Library of Congress,
p. 25; City of Minneapolis, p. 27; Minnesota Department of Jobs
and Training, pp. 31, 42; U.S. Army, p. 33; Minneapolis Department
of Public Works, pp. 34, 53; LeeAnne Engfer, p. 39; Tennessee
Valley Authority, p. 48; Norwest Corporation, p. 50; Apple Valley
High School, p. 55 (bottom); J.L. Snyder, p. 57; U.S. Capitol His-
torical Society, p. 61; Pepperidge Farm, p. 63; United States Treasury
Department, pp. 67, 71; National Archives, pp. 73, 75 (both);
Dictionary of American Portraits, p. 74; Minnesota DFL, p. 79;
Michael Evans/The White House, p. 80 (upper left); Department
of Defense, p. 80 (right).

Front cover photograph: NASA. Back cover photograph: LeeAnne
Engfer.